Three spotty monsters are
up in a balloon.

Three spotty monsters are
flying to the moon.

Three spotty monsters are waving to a train.

Three spotty monsters are
waving to a plane.

Three spotty monsters are
waving to the stars.

Three spotty monsters are
flying off to Mars.